The Busy Bee

The Busy Bee

V. Gilbert Beers

Illustrated by Tonda Rae Nalle

VICTOR BOOKS
A DIVISION OF SCRIPTURE PRESS PUBLICATIONS INC.
USA CANADA ENGLAND

Copyright © 1994 by Educational Publishing Concepts, Inc., Wheaton, Illinois

Text © 1994 by V. Gilbert Beers

All right reserved. Written permission must be secured from the publisher to use or reproduce any part of this book, except for brief quotations in critical reviews or articles.

Published in Wheaton, Illinois by Victor Books/SP Publications, Inc., Wheaton, Illinois.

ISBN 1-56476-313-7

Printed in the United States of America
1 2 3 4 5 6 7 8 9 10 - 98 97 96 95 94

TO PARENTS AND TEACHERS

What does your child do when a problem comes along? How does she respond to it? Where does he find the solution?

What we need is a good role model—someone who faces problems as we do, but knows the right way to resolve them. The Muffin Family is a role-model family. They face problems much like the ones that bother us daily. But there's a difference. The Muffins are not quite like their neighbors. You will soon learn that they are Christians, and thus they meet their problems with Bible truth.

The Muffins aren't perfect. Neither are you and I. But they are Christian. They aren't free from problems. But they resolve them—God's Way.

If you're looking for a book that will role-model Bible truth at work in a family much like yours, meet The Muffin Family.

V. Gilbert Beers

"Mini, will you help me get the dinner dishes on the table?" Mommi called from the kitchen.

"Maybe," said Mini.

Mommi Muffin said nothing more. After she had finished making the tossed salad, she put the dinner dishes on the table herself.

But Mini was so interested in her book that maybe never happened. At last Mommi called Poppi and Maxi herself.

After dinner, Mommi called Mini again. "Would you like to help me with the dishes now?" she asked.

"Maybe," said Mini.

"Maybe, maybe, maybe," Mommi told Poppi when Mini had gone to get some things ready for school the next day. "That's all I've heard lately."

Maxi overheard what Mommi said and wanted to offer his opinion. "I'd give her a time out, that's what I'd do," he said importantly. "No kid of mine is going to 'maybe' me."

When Poppi heard that, he had to hold the newspaper higher so Maxi would not see him chuckling.

"I wanted to give her at least three time outs this evening," said Mommi. "But more than that, I want her to WANT to help the family."

Poppi put down the newspaper. "Seems to me we have two lady bees buzzing around our house," he said. "As long as you're willing to be the busy bee, Mini will be willing to be the MAY-be."

Mommi was quiet for a while as she thought about that. "You're right!" she said. "Perhaps I need to become the MAY-be until Mini learns to become a busy bee, too."

Mommi had just finished saying that when Mini came running out of her room.

"Mommi, I need a button sewed on my dress for school tomorrow," she said. "Will you do that for me?"

"Maybe," Mommi said softly.

"Maybe?" Mini repeated, her mouth dropping open. "But I need my button sewed on. Don't you want to do it?"

"Maybe," Mommi said again.

Mini stood with her mouth wide open, staring at Mommi. This wasn't like her. Poppi hid his face behind the newspaper so Mini would not see him chuckling. Maxi quickly went into the kitchen so Mini wouldn't see him laughing. Mommi kept on looking through her magazine.

Mini walked sadly back to her room and got a needle and thread. It wasn't easy to put a button on.

She lost the button twice and almost stomped her foot when she had to thread the needle a second time. But at last she got the button sewed on.

Mini looked sad as she walked out to the living room again. Mommi was still looking through the magazine.

"Mommi, you…I mean we…that is, I have to make my lunch for school tomorrow," Mini said. "Will you help me?"

Mommi turned a page in the magazine without looking at Mini.
"Maybe," she said.

Mini stood there for a while, waiting for Mommi to come with her. But Mommi kept on looking through the magazine.

At last, Mini walked sadly to the kitchen and made her lunch. Some tears began to trickle down her cheek. Mommi had never said "maybe" to her before. She had always said, "I'll be glad to help you, Mini."

Mini thought about the maybes as she put her sandwich in the lunch box and washed an apple.

Then she remembered all the maybes she had said to Mommi lately. She knew now how much a maybe hurts when someone really needs help.

When Mini had tucked her lunch box into the refrigerator, she went to her closet to get her clothes ready for school the next day. Her dress HAD to be ironed.

Mini carried her dress to the living room and stood next to Mommi's chair. She didn't know what to say to Mommi now, or how to ask Mommi to help her.

"Maybe," Mommi said before Mini could ask.

Mini burst into tears and threw her arms around Mommi.

"Oh, Mommi, please don't ever say that word to me again," she sobbed. "I'm sorry I said it to you. I won't maybe you anymore."

Mommi gave Mini a big hug and dried her tears. "Let's both be busy bees for each other instead of MAY-bes," said Mommi. "I think that's the way God wants families to be."

"You mean B-E-E, don't you, Mommi?" Mini said with a giggle.

Then Mommi and Mini both had a good laugh as they went to get the ironing board. And Poppi could put his newspaper down and laugh with them.